Now, Now, Markus

Library of Congress Cataloging-in-Publication Data
Auer, Martin.   [Bimbo]
Now, now, Markus / Martin Auer and Simone Klages.
p.   cm.
"First published in the Federal Republic of Germany in 1988 under
the title Bimbo"—T.p. verso.
Summary: When his parents disapprove of his pet swan,
Markus and the swan run away into the woods
where they encounter a giant.
ISBN 0-688-08974-7.   ISBN 0-688-08975-5 (lib. bdg.)
[1. Swans—Fiction.   2. Pets—Fiction.
3. Giants—Fiction.]   I. Klages, Simone.   II. Title.
PZ7.A911No 1989   [E]—dc19   88-34320   CIP   AC

NOW, NOW, MARKUS

by Martin Auer
and Simone Klages

Greenwillow Books, New York

One day Markus said to his parents,

"I want a bird!"

"Oh, my goodness,"
   said his mother.

"Now, now, now,"
   said his father.

"A beautiful bird,
   but not in a cage!"

"Oh, my goodness,"
   said his mother.

"Now, now, now,"
   said his father.

"My bird will sleep with me,

and eat breakfast with me," said Markus.

"Oh, my goodness," said his mother.
"Now, now, now," said his father.

"Do I get a bird or don't I?" asked Markus.

"I won't have a bird
in the house,"
said his mother.

"And certainly not
without a cage,"
said his father.

"Fine," said Markus.
"Then I will
drop dead."

And he did.

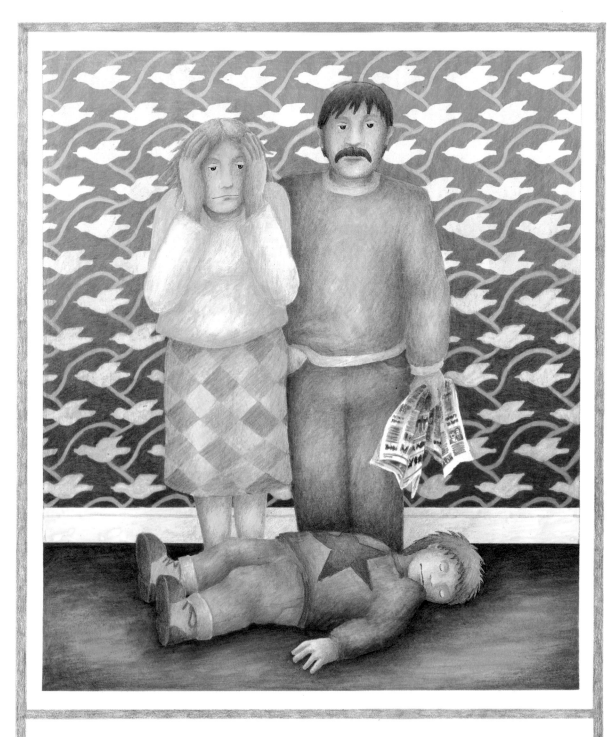

"Oh, my goodness," said his mother.
"Now, now, now," said his father.

"Well, do I get a bird or not?"
asked Markus,
lying dead on the floor.

"Well, I guess so," said his mother.
"But in a cage," said his father.

So Markus came back to life
and went out to get a bird.

He was back in an hour.

"Where's your bird?"
asked his father.

"I hope it won't smell,"
said his mother."

"He's coming," said Markus.

And in came the bird.
It was a beautiful white swan.

"Oh, my goodness," said his mother.
"Now, now, now," said his father.

"Here is my bird," said Markus.

"That swan is not coming into my house,"
said his mother.

"Swans belong outside," said his father.

"Fine," said Markus. "I will drop dead."
And he did.

"Stop all this nonsense," said his mother.

"It won't help," said his father.

"I'm dead," said Markus.

"Dead boys
don't get supper,"
said his mother.

"And if you're dead
you don't need a bird,"
said his father.

"Very well," said Markus. "We'll go and live in the woods." And he got up and left.

"Oh, my goodness," said his mother.

"Now, now, now," said his father.

And the swan followed Markus out the door.

It was almost dark when Markus
reached the woods.

"There's a stranger coming," hooted the owl.

"Someone who doesn't belong here," hissed the snake.

"Someone we don't like," growled the fox.

"Someone who frightens me," wailed the hare.

"We'll chase him away," hooted the owl.
"Yes, get rid of him," hissed the snake.
"Make sure he never comes back,"
growled the fox.
"So that he can't hurt me," wailed the hare.

"Should I peck
his eyes out?"
hooted the owl,
fluttering his wings.

"Shall I poison him?"
hissed the snake,
sticking out his tongue.

"Shall I bite
his legs?"
growled the fox,
baring his teeth.

"I can't stand
the sight of blood,"
wailed the hare,
and he jumped
into his hole.

Just then the swan caught up with Markus.

"Oh, dear, he's not alone," hooted the owl.
"He has a mighty protector,"
hissed the snake.
"What will we do?" growled the fox.
"Will he hurt us?" wailed the hare.

And Markus said, "Oh, just be quiet!"
Then he lay down and went to sleep,

and the swan covered him with his wing.

The moon rose and moved across the sky.
And Markus slept.

The moon set. And Markus slept.
Then the sky grew light
and the sun rose.

Markus woke up and said to the swan,
"Come on. We're going to find a giant."

And off they went.

It wasn't long before they found the giant. "Hey, giant," called Markus.

"Yes?" roared the giant,
rolling his eyes.

"We've been looking for you," said Markus.

"So I noticed,"
roared the giant.

"Aren't you afraid of us?" asked Markus.

"Me? Afraid? Ha! You're the
one who should be afraid!"
roared the giant.

"But I have a mighty protector," said Markus.

The giant laughed. "I'll
eat him for breakfast—
and you, too!"

"We'll see about that," said Markus.

The giant grabbed Markus and the swan
and swallowed them in one gulp.

"Delicious," he said, smacking his lips.
Then he burped, and all the flowers wilted.

Inside the giant,
the swan fluttered his wings.

The giant's stomach began to growl.

"I feel terrible," he sighed,
rolling his eyes.

"That was not a good breakfast at all,"
the giant complained.
"I feel sick," he wailed.
The growling and rumbling in his stomach
grew worse and worse.
The giant began to shake.
His mouth opened
and *SCHWAPP*—
Markus was out.
And *SCHWAPP*—
the swan followed.

And *SCHWAPP*—everything else the giant
had recently eaten followed the swan:

Children and bicycles and watchdogs
and wristwatches and racing cars
and soap bubbles and circuses
and dormice and doormats and dormitories
and chestnut trees and doughnut stands
and laughter and liveries and liberties
and leap years and thunderstorms
and canaries and canopies and can openers
and candies and cannonballs and soda pop
and French fries and fresh flies
and ice cream and nice dreams and five screams
and riverbeds and flower beds
and flower pots and hippopotami
and drainpipes and hornpipes
and secrets and miracles
and a little elf in a little box
and a drawerful of socks
and Turkish delight and a murky night
and puppies and poppies
and peacocks and guinea pigs
and turtles and turtledoves

and moles and buttonholes
and parakeets and parachutes
and parrots and carrots
and ants and pants and panting aunts

and flesh-eating plants
and a honeybee
and
a funny flea.

"Fine," said Markus.
"Now we can go home."

"I'm back," said Markus.

"Just look at you!" said his mother.
"Get into the tub this minute!"

"An owl almost
pecked my eyes out,"
said Markus.

"Do what your mother says," said his father.

 "A snake almost
poisoned me,"
said Markus.

"And give me your dirty clothes so I can
wash them," said his mother.

"And a fox almost
bit my legs,"
said Markus.

"Do what your mother says," said his father.
"And a giant swallowed me," said Markus.
"Of course," said his mother.
"Naturally," said his father.

"But my brave swan protected me and
tickled the giant until he spat me out,
and my life was saved. And that's why
my brave swan must stay with me—
or I'll drop dead," said Markus.

"Well, we'll see," said his father.
"If you're good," said his mother.

"And may all the others that were inside
the giant come and live with me too?"
asked Markus.

"Yes, yes, but now get into the tub,"
said his mother.

So they all came in—all the children and
bicycles and watchdogs and wristwatches and
racing cars and soap bubbles and circuses and
dormice and doormats and dormitories
and chestnut trees and doughnut stands
and laughter and liveries and liberties and
leap years and thunderstorms and
canaries and canopies and can openers
and candies and cannonballs and soda pop
and French fries and fresh flies and
ice cream and nice dreams and five screams

and riverbeds and flower beds and flower pots
and hippopotami and drainpipes and hornpipes
and secrets and miracles and a little elf in a little box
and a drawerful of socks and Turkish delight
and a murky night and puppies and poppies
and peacocks and guinea pigs and turtles and
turtledoves and moles and buttonholes and
parakeets and parachutes and parrots and
carrots and ants and pants and panting aunts and
flesh-eating plants and a honeybee
and the funny flea.

They all marched into Markus's room,
and the flea closed the door behind them.

"Oh, my goodness," said Markus's mother.
"Now, now, now," said his father.

"And now I'll take my bath," said Markus.